The Wild Baby
Goes to Sea

by BARBRO LINDGREN

pictures by EVA ERIKSSON

adapted from the Swedish by

JACK PRELUTSKY

Greenwillow Books

New York

JEFFERSONVILLE TOWNSHIP PUBLIC LIBRARY
JEFFERSONVILLE, INDIANA

AUG   1983

j
e
L7462W

Swedish text copyright © 1982
by Barbro Lindgren
Illustrations copyright © 1982
by Eva Eriksson
English text copyright © 1983
by Jack Prelutsky
Swedish edition entitled
Den vilda Bebiresan
published by Rabén & Sjögren

All rights reserved. No part of
this book may be reproduced or
utilized in any form or by any
means, electronic or mechanical,
including photocopying, recording
or by any information storage and
retrieval system, without permission
in writing from the Publisher,
Greenwillow Books, a division of
William Morrow & Company, Inc.,
105 Madison Avenue, New York,
N.Y. 10016.

Printed in the
United States of America
First American Edition
10 9 8 7 6 5 4 3 2 1

Library of Congress Cataloging
in Publication Data

Lindgren, Barbro.
The wild baby goes to sea.
Translation of: Den vilda bebiresan.
Summary: While his mother cleans
house, rambunctious baby Ben
sets sail in a wooden box and
has many adventures.
[1. Mothers and sons—Fiction.
2. Stories in rhyme]
I. Eriksson, Eva, ill.   II. Title.
PZ8.3.L616Wj 1983   [E]   82-15623
ISBN 0-688-01960-9
ISBN 0-688-01961-7 (lib. bdg.)

8305945 ℓ

Baby Ben was twice as wild
as any other ten,
there never was another child
as wild as baby Ben.
He loved to run, to jump and climb,
he was in trouble half the time.

One calm and quiet afternoon,
while mama worked and hummed a tune,
a notion came into his head,
"I think I'll build a boat," he said.
He found a box, and one, two, three,
he had a boat to sail the sea.

He took on board
his little crew,
Mouse, Giraffe,
and Bunny too.

Then dumped in buns,
a tasty treat,
that they might have
a bite to eat.

He borrowed mama's apron then,
a splendid sail, thought baby Ben.
Exactly what I need today
to help my sailboat sail away.

Mama shouted high and clear,
"Goodbye! Goodbye! Be careful, dear!"

No sooner had they sailed from shore
than waves began to churn and roar.
The crewmates three were terrified,
"We're scared! We're sick! We're soaked!" they cried.
But baby Ben munched on a bun.
"What fun!" He laughed. "What lovely fun!"

The sailboat lurched, and suddenly
poor Mouse fell out into the sea.

But baby Ben tossed out some string
and saved the frightened little thing.

A hungry fish climbed up the side,
"I'm going to eat you up!" he cried.

But little Mouse and baby Ben
threw buns at that old fish,
until it headed off again
inside a baking dish.

A rooster came into their view,
"Help! Help!" he crowed. "I'm in a stew,
I never learned to swim or float,
please take me in your little boat."

Then baby Ben,
without a word,
reached out and saved
the dripping bird.
The grateful rooster
took his beak
and pecked Ben lightly
on the cheek.

They sailed up north,
they sailed down south,
they sailed into
a whale's great mouth.

It was strange inside that whale,
they all felt cold, they all grew pale.
But steering boldly, baby Ben
soon had them back outside again.

A storm came up, the ocean swelled,
"Oh, save us, please!" the rooster yelled.
But baby Ben was undismayed,
he chuckled as they pitched and swayed.

The sailboat tossed,
the sailboat bobbed
as Mouse, Giraffe,
and Bunny sobbed.

The sailboat floundered upside down,
the rooster screamed, "We're going to drown!"
But baby Ben said, "Oh, what fun!"
and saved his crewmates, one by one.

(He even saved a bun or two
to feed his scared and soaking crew.)

Giraffe and Bunny moaned and wailed,
"We wish that we had never sailed!"
But Mouse and Ben had quite a laugh
when they heard Bunny and Giraffe.

The sea grew still, the moon appeared
as something gruesome, dark, and weird
arose from underneath the sea
and crooned, "Come here and follow me."
"No, thank you, sir," said baby Ben.
"It's time that we were home again."

They heard a tick, they heard a tock,
they saw their friendly wooden clock,
and knew that they were back on shore,
safe and sound on mama's floor.

And mama was delighted too
to see her baby and his crew.

But still, she wondered
all that day
just how that rooster
came their way!

LINDGREN, BARBRO
THE WILD BABY GOES TO SEA
je   L7462w   83-05945

JEFFERSONVILLE TWP PUBLIC LIBRARY

3 1861 00043 6376

J ● L7462w
Lindgren, Barbro. The wild baby
goes to sea /
Greenwillow Books, c1983. 1st A

Jeffersonville Township Public
Library
P.O. Box 1548
Jeffersonville, IN 47131

DEMCO